This book belongs to

Light up!

YUNMIE KIM

Once there was a firefly named Finto.

He loved pollen stew,

and a cup of honey tea
after that.

But there was something
he loved more than pollen or honey.

It was helping his dear friends.

His bright glow was helpful for many others,
so it always kept him busy.

Everything was good until one evening,
when Finto's bottom wouldn't light up.

He tried shaking the light on.

Paff!

He tried blowing the light on.

He even tried
plunging the light on.

But no matter how hard he tried,
his light wouldn't come back.

Finto was very worried.

"Finto!"

Over in the field,
Finto's minibeast friends waved at him.

"Do you wanna play a game with us?"
asked the minibeasts.

"Sorry, but I'm quite
busy right now" replied Finto.
"Oh, what's up?" asked
the minibeasts.

Finto explained he had lost his light
and now that he was worried he wouldn't be able to
help his friends anymore.

Finto gave a deep sigh.
His friends understood why he was worried.

The minibeasts shared lots of ideas
for bringing Finto's light back.

Finto wasn't very sure that the ideas would work.

"I think you should try a candle," said Bobo the Bumblebee, "It's beautiful and relaxing to watch."

Bobo brought a candle and put it on Finto's head.
It looked great there.

But, soon...

Aaaww!

...the candle started dripping all over Finto
and it was very hot!

"I think you should use a torch," said Stamba
the Stag beetle, "It's really bright and safe to use."

He taped a torch around Finto's tummy
and switched on.

A bright beam shone across Finto's face.
It made him look very spooky.

"Why don't you try fairy lights? suggested Dami the Damselfly, "You'll look like a beautiful Christmas tree!"

Dami decorated Finto with fairy lights
and he looked magnificent!

But, wait!

Help!

The fairy lights tangled around Finto and he fell over.
Thump!

Finto sat down for a little rest.
His neck was tired.
His skin was sore.
His bottom was bruised.
But he still had no light.

A little tear came to his eyes.

"Cheer up, Finto" said Bobo.

"We'll find a way to bring your light back" said Stamba.

"Even if you don't light up, you're still our friend" said Dami.

Everyone gave Finto a hug.
He smiled and hugged them back.

They all heard a very strange noise
which came from Finto's tummy.

Everyone started laughing.

"It must be time to eat," said Finto scratching his head,
"Let's go and have dinner."

They had a wonderful meal together.

Finto was so hungry that he gobbled down his pollen stew and drank his honey tea in one gulp. He began to feel quite full.

"Finto, look! You're shiny again!" Dami shouted out.

There it was!
A little light was coming back to Finto's bottom.

And it soon turned into a dazzling glow!

Finto was very happy.
Everyone celebrated by singing and dancing around him.

Now, the sky was dark.
Finto jumped up and soared high
to help his friends find their way back home.

That evening,
Finto's light was brighter than ever before.

A WORD FROM THE AUTHOR

Every year, we're losing butterflies, moths,
dragonflies, bees, beetles, crickets, and many more.

Studies show over 40% of insect species are in danger of
extinction and flying insects have decliend by more than 75%
over the course of just 27 years.

Bugs can be occasional nuisances, but they play many important
roles on Earth. They visit flowers to help them make seeds. They
become food to animals like birds and frogs. They support our
farmers by eating up pests on vegetables and grains. And there's
a lot more. Without their help, we won't survive.

Find out more about the endangered insects and meet the
adorable minibeast characters on the website:
www.yoomsworld.com

MORE TO READ

Luna Moth

Molly the moth is forever drawn to the bright,
beautiful glow of the Moon. She tries hard to
get close to him but this never seems to work,
which makes her sad. Then one day Molly gets
an unexpected visitor...

Printed in Great Britain
by Amazon